Frosty the Snowman

Adapted by Diane Muldrow
Illustrated by Josie Yee

A Golden Book ❄ New York
Golden Books Publishing Company, Inc., New York, New York 10106

It all started with the snow, the first snow of the season.

As every child knows, there's a certain magic to the very first snow. And when it falls on the day before Christmas, something wonderful is bound to happen!

"Children, back to your seats!" called the teacher. "The snow can wait. I've hired Professor Hinkle, the magician, to entertain us for our Christmas party!"

Unfortunately, Professor Hinkle was just about the worst magician in the world.

"... And so I put the eggs into my
magic hat," said Professor Hinkle.
"Abracadabra! And *voilà*, the eggs have turned into ... a mess.
Where is my rabbit? Hocus Pocus, where are you?"
    He didn't know that his rabbit, Hocus Pocus,
was hiding in the hat.

"The only thing that this hat is good for is the trash can!" said Professor Hinkle.

But the hat didn't stay there for long. The hat—with Hocus Pocus underneath—hopped out of the trash can and out the door! That's when the bell rang. The children were free for the whole Christmas holiday!

"Hey, look at the snow!" cried the children as they ran outside. They worked together to build the first snowman of the season.

Once the children had given him eyes, a nose, and a mouth, it was time to name him.

"How about Frosty?" asked Karen. "Frosty the Snowman!"

The children began to sing:

"*Frosty the Snowman, was a jolly, happy soul*
with a corn cob pipe, and a button nose,
and two eyes made out of coal."

"Come back here, you!" cried Professor Hinkle, chasing Hocus Pocus. Suddenly, a gust of wind blew the hat up into the air—and onto Frosty's head!

"Happy Birthday!" said the snowman.

Karen gasped and said, "That hat brought Frosty to life. It must be magic!"

When Professor Hinkle heard that, he took the hat back!

"But it's not yours anymore," protested Karen. "You threw it away."

"This hat will make me a millionaire!" said the greedy magician. Off he went to make his fortune.

Hocus Pocus felt that the hat really did belong to Frosty. So he hop, hop, hopped back to Frosty and the children as fast as he could to return the magic hat.

"Happy Birthday!" said Frosty again, as soon as the hat was placed on his head.

"Hey, I said my first words. I'm alive! What a neat thing to happen to a nice guy like me!"

There must have been some magic
    in that old silk hat they found,
For when they placed it on his head
    he began to dance around!
Frosty the Snowman was alive as he could be.
And the children say he could laugh and play
    just the same as you and me.

When the sun peeked out from behind the clouds, Frosty exclaimed, "Oh, I'm all wishy-washy! I'm starting to melt!"

The children knew they needed to take Frosty someplace where he'd never melt—like the chilly North Pole. They decided to go to the railroad station and find a train for Frosty.

"Let's have a parade through town!" shouted Frosty. "Come on kids, follow the leader!"

All too soon it was time for the train, and Frosty, to leave.

"I'll go with you, Frosty," said Karen. "I'm sure I'll be back in time for supper."

Karen, Frosty, and Hocus Pocus jumped into a refrigerated boxcar on a freight train headed north.

No one saw Professor Hinkle sneak under the train car and hold on.

A refrigerated boxcar is a splendid way to travel. Splendid, that is, if one is a snowman, or a furry-coated rabbit. But for a little girl like Karen, it was just too cold.

So when the little freight train made a quick stop, Frosty got them all out.

No one saw Professor Hinkle jump off, too.

Frosty took Karen and Hocus Pocus to a wooded glen, where they found the animals decorating the trees for their big celebration. They knew Santa Claus was to come that night!

After Hocus Pocus spoke to the animals, they agreed to build a campfire to keep Karen warm.

But it didn't take long for Professor Hinkle to catch up with the friends.

"Get on my shoulders, Karen!" cried Frosty.

Frosty, since he was made of snow, was the fastest belly-whopper in the world. Soon he and Karen were sliding down a hill, leaving that greedy Professor Hinkle far behind.

At the bottom of the hill was a tiny greenhouse for growing tropical poinsettias for Christmas. It was the perfect place for Karen to stay warm.

"But, Frosty, you'll melt in here!" said Karen.

"I'll only stay inside for a minute," Frosty assured her.

But that nasty Professor Hinkle once again caught up with them and locked the door, trapping the friends inside!

That night, Hocus Pocus led Santa Claus to the greenhouse to save Frosty. But by then, poor Frosty had melted completely.

"Don't cry, Karen," said Santa kindly. "Frosty's not gone for good. He was made out of Christmas snow. You can bet your boots that when a good, jolly December wind kisses it, it'll turn into Christmas snow all over again. Just watch!"

Santa opened the door, and when the wind whirled in and out, Frosty was back!

Santa was about to place the magic hat on Frosty's head when Professor Hinkle shouted, "I want that hat, and I want it now!"

Santa replied, "If you touch this hat, I'll never bring you another Christmas present. Go home right now and write 'I am very sorry for what I did to Frosty' a hundred zillion times. Then maybe, just maybe, you'll find something in your stocking tomorrow morning."

Professor Hinkle was very sorry indeed. He ran straight home to start writing and hoped that Santa would, just maybe, bring him a new hat for Christmas.

"Happy Birthday!" said Frosty once more.

Karen was happy to see her friend again. But now it was time to go home. Santa put Karen in his sleigh and promised her that he would take Frosty back to the North Pole with him.

Karen hated to say good-bye to Frosty, but as Santa
promised, Frosty returned every year with the magical
Christmas snow. And every year, the town celebrated with
a big Christmas party.

Frosty the Snowman
    had to hurry on his way.
But he waved good-bye,
    saying, "Don't you cry,
    I'll be back on Christmas Day."